Frozen Solid
at
SILVER STREET
FARM

Frozen Solid at SILVER STREET FARM

NICOLA DAVIES
illustrated by Katharine McEwen

WALKER
BOOKS

First published 2012 by Walker Books Ltd
87 Vauxhall Walk, London SE11 5HJ

2 4 6 8 10 9 7 5 3 1

Text © 2012 Nicola Davies
Illustrations © 2012 Katharine McEwen

The right of Nicola Davies and Katharine McEwen to be identified as author and illustrator respectively of this work has been asserted by them in accordance with the Copyright, Designs and Patents Act 1988.

This book has been typeset in Stempel Schneidler and Cows

Printed and bound in Great Britain
by Clays Ltd, St Ives plc

British Library Cataloguing in Publication Data:
a catalogue record for this book is available from the British Library

ISBN 978-1-4063-3783-9

www.walker.co.uk

For the first big Silver Street fans,
Jemma, Isabel, Sam, Olly, Winnie and Daphne

A MAP OF

W

MAIN GATE

GOATS

FLORA'S OFFICE

VI

SHEEP

DUCK HOUSE

TURKEYS

DAIRY

FEED STORE

TURKEY PEN

CHICKEN HOUSE

FEED STORE

PIG

Chapter One

The Silver Street ducks couldn't understand it. Overnight the water in the canal had gone hard. So instead of jumping off their little jetty and paddling about, they slid and slipped, their webbed feet skidding from under them, sending them sprawling on their tummies or head first onto their beaks.

Meera, Karl and Gemma, the three children who had started Silver Street City Farm, couldn't help giggling as they watched the ducks skating and tobogganing on the frozen surface.

"I know I shouldn't really laugh at them," said Gemma, throwing another scoop of food onto the ice for the ducks, "but they look so funny..."

Chinook the Canada goose and her little flock of friends noticed it was feeding time. They skidded over to where the ducks were gobbling up the grain, and landed in a tangle of long necks and wings.

When the children had recovered from another fit of the giggles, Karl poked the ice with a stick. "Do you think it's thick enough to stand on?" he wondered.

"Only if you're a duck!" teased Meera.

"This is Lonchester, Karl," Gemma laughed. "Not the Arctic!"

The girls walked off to do other chores, but Karl hung back, looking dreamily at the frozen canal. He longed to go skating outdoors, the way his Auntie Nat had when she was a little girl in Russia. But Lonchester winters were never cold enough.

"It'll probably melt by the afternoon," Karl said gloomily to himself, and stomped off to join the girls.

But the ice didn't melt. In fact it got colder and colder. By the third day of what the local papers had begun to call "The Big Freeze", weather forecasters were saying it was the coldest snap that Lonchester had ever known. The Christmas holidays were extended as many schools had frozen pipes. Children all over the city celebrated and looked up into the clear skies hoping for snow to follow the ice. Grown-ups all over the city looked down, so as not to slip on the ice slides that the children had made.

By the tenth day of the freeze, slowly but surely Lonchester began to shut down. The roads were too icy for driving and the pavements too slippery for walking. Lorries could not deliver to shops and the supermarket shelves started to empty. The big power station that made all of Lonchester's electricity stuttered like a failing light bulb, so that there were power cuts at all hours of the day and night.

Flora, the Silver Street farm manager, bought a digital thermometer to measure just how cold it was getting on the farm. Every day it showed a lower temperature.

"Minus fifteen degrees last night!" Flora

announced one morning when the children arrived at the farm to help. Karl found himself thinking surely *that* must have made the ice thick enough to skate on. But there was no time to find out. It had become so cold that simply getting clean water to all the Silver Street animals was a struggle, because it turned to ice in minutes. Warm water had to be delivered to all the pens twice or even three times a day so the animals had a chance to drink before it froze, and they all seemed to be eating twice as much, just to stay warm! Karl, Meera and Gemma, together with their friends Bish Bosh and his little brother Squirt (home from Hollywood where he had been starring in a film), were kept very, very busy. And very, very happy, as spending extra time at Silver Street was all they ever wanted to do.

The Big Freeze felt like a Big Adventure to the children. Silver Street Farm looked like a magical kingdom, sparkling with frost and decorated with icicles, and it seemed that the cold was making magical things happen too. Late one afternoon Flora called everyone to the farmyard, where hundreds of small, wild birds were hopping about, collecting bits of fallen animal food. The birds took no notice of humans walking among them. They even pecked food from the children's hands.

"They're as tame as budgies!" Bish Bosh exclaimed as a robin sat on his palm.

"They're so cold and hungry they can't be bothered to be scared any more," said Meera.

The children couldn't help smiling as birds fluttered around, perching fearlessly on their heads and shoulders.

But Auntie Nat wasn't smiling. "Hmmm," she said. "I see wild birds tame in winter like this before. Long ago in Russia. It is not a good sign." She shook her head inside her big furry hat, and waggled her woolly gloved fingers in warning, but no one took any notice.

Chapter Two

Gemma's House — 7.15a.m.

Gemma reached out to switch off her beeping alarm. Brrrrr! It was so cold outside her bed! She pulled her arm back into the warm and peeked out between the cosy folds of duvet. For a moment, she thought that she must be seeing things. There were huge icicles hanging from a big black crack in her ceiling, and her radiator was sprouting a frozen waterfall of ice. She could hear her brother Kevin shouting from the bathroom. He sounded very fed up.

"Dad!" Kevin yelled. "The taps won't turn on!"

"The pipes have frozen, son," Dad called back from the bottom of the stairs, "and the electric's off too."

A moment later, Gemma was doing some yelling of her own, as the ceiling of her bedroom stopped being a ceiling and decided there was a future for it as a floor.

Karl's Flat — 8.10a.m.

Karl was wrapped in his duvet, wearing all the clothes he could fit on his body. He peered out of the seventeenth-floor window of the little flat he shared with Auntie Nat. All he could see was white. Clouds had gathered in the night and were now dumping their load of snow on Lonchester.

Auntie Nat emerged from the kitchen carrying a single lighted candle that flickered and sent mysterious shadows dancing all around the room.

"Look at the snow, Auntie!" Karl beamed excitedly.

Auntie Nat made her most disapproving noise. "Nnnnnhh," she said. "This is not fun, Karl. There is no water, no electricity. We cannot stay here."

Meera's House — 8.45a.m.

Meera's parents were loading their car with blankets and food, whilst her little brothers, Sadar, Dayal and Etash, were jumping up and down on the snowy pavement. The family were going to Uncle Sanjay's house, out of town. Uncle Sanjay had a wood-burning stove and generator. But Meera didn't want to go.

"Mum, please let me stay at Silver Street," she pleaded.

"For the last time," Mrs Gupta said, "no. Look up and down this road, Meera. Everyone is leaving."

Mrs Gupta was right. Temperatures as cold as the Arctic had caused everything to break down. There were power cuts all over town and some places didn't have water. Now the heaviest snow on record was forecast. Lonchester's "Big Freeze" had become "An Emergency" and lots of people had decided to leave before the snow trapped them.

"But Mu-umm…" Meera almost wailed. She couldn't bear the thought of being stranded at Uncle Sanjay's, when Silver Street might need her.

Her father came to the rescue. "Meera'll be bored at Sanjay's," he said kindly to his wife. "She'll be fine at Silver Street, dear heart. She can take a sleeping bag and blankets. Besides, this weather will pass in a day or two."

"Oh, OK then," said Mrs Gupta reluctantly. "I will give Flora a call."

Lonchester Children's Home — 9.10a.m.

Bish Bosh and Squirt didn't like playing a dirty trick on Dave and Sarah, who looked after them, but as Bish Bosh pointed out solemnly, "These are extreme circumstances."

They had got onto the bus that was taking them out of town and pretended to go to sleep at the back. Dave ticked their names off the list, while Sarah got all the other children on board. But just before the bus pulled away, when the aisle was piled so high with luggage that no one could even see the back seat, they slipped out through the emergency exit, ran back inside the house and hid.

"By the time they notice," Bish Bosh said as they crouched behind the sofa, "there'll be too much snow for them to turn back!"

Squirt grinned and touched his palm to his brother's in a silent high five.

Silver Street Farm — 10.23a.m.

Flora had never seen snow like it, not even on the Scottish farm where she grew up. The paths she had cleared half an hour before were filling up.

"If it carries on like this," she said to herself,

"it'll be over the windows by teatime!"

She put the shovel back inside. She would have to wade through the snow to get to the animals, even if it took all day. Just as she was wondering if she should make a pair of snowshoes out of a couple of old tennis rackets, six figures appeared out of the whiteness, like ghosts. They wore hats and gloves and boots, and were covered from head to foot in snow.

"Hello, Flora," said one of the snowpeople in Meera's voice. "We've come to stay!"

Chapter Three

Auntie Nat knew about this kind of weather, so she took command and organized them like a platoon of soldiers. The snow could go on falling for hours, she told them, so there was no point trying to clear it away. Anyway, snow was a good insulator. The thickening layer of snow on the roof of the office and the animals' houses would help to keep them warm.

"So, all we can do today" said Auntie Nat, "is give animals food, put their water inside their sleeping place so it won't freeze and look at them again when snow stops."

She told everyone to keep gloves and hats on all the time: "You will get frostbite on bare skin," she warned, pointing to Flora's thermometer. "Look! It is minus 16 degrees!"

Bish Bosh and Squirt piled logs and bits of old wood right outside the door of the office, so they would be able to keep the stove going easily. In the dairy, Flora wrapped her precious goat's cheeses so that the frost wouldn't spoil them. And Auntie Nat moved cooking things and food from the little kitchen where she made snacks for visitors into the office, so they could cook on the woodburner.

Meanwhile Gemma, Meera and Karl had the hardest job, taking food and water to all the animals, struggling through the snow with heavy buckets and nets of hay. It was hard to see more than a metre ahead in the swirling flakes, and the thick white coating changed the way the farm looked so much that it was sometimes hard to recognize where they were. At times, they felt that they were lost in the eerie whiteness all around them.

Silver Street's newest animals, the alpacas, Tika and Kusi, seemed quite excited by the snow. Their wool-framed faces, one cream and one black, peeked out over the half-door of their stall. They made little humming noises and sniffed at the snow. Their thick coats were clearly keeping out the cold and they didn't really want to be shut in at all.

"We'll let you out when it stops snowing," Meera promised as the top half of their door swung shut.

All the other animals seemed to understand instinctively that the best thing to do was keep warm and sleep until things got better. The pigs hardly opened their eyes when their food arrived, and the rabbits and guinea pigs were really just wiggly shapes underneath their straw. The sheep were lying with their skinny legs tucked under them, so they looked like big blobs of cotton wool. Even the goats seemed quite cosy, cuddled in the corner of their stall.

"It's well above freezing in here, the same as all the other stalls," said Karl, checking the temperature on the thermometer.

"Great," said Gemma. "So their water won't freeze."

"But I might," shivered Meera. "Come on, guys. Let's feed the chickens and get indoors. I'm sooo cold!"

Outside, the light was fading and the whiteness of the falling snow was turning grey. The children couldn't make out the shape of the old signal box that was the Silver Street chicken house until they were almost on top of it.

"It's got a lot of snow on its roof!" said Karl. "I hope the stilts can take the weight!"

The words were hardly out of his mouth when there was a horrible *crraaack*! One of the stilts holding up the chicken house snapped like a twig and the whole thing began to topple and then to fall. The three friends had to throw themselves into the snow to get out of the way as it came crashing down.

The children spat snow out of their mouths and stood up. The signal box looked as if it had exploded. It had shattered into matchsticks and the sound of terrified squawking was coming from all around. The chickens had been catapulted through the air and had landed in the soft snow unhurt but very scared.

Meera, Karl and Gemma began to rescue the frightened hens. They picked them, clucking, out of the powdery snow, put them gently into a sack and then ferried them in batches to the goat stall, to perch on top of the straw bales.

But soon the grey dusk turned to darkness and the wind began to whip the snow into a blizzard.

"We'll have to stop," said Meera. "I can hardly see a thing any more."

"But we haven't found Sean and Fluff yet!" Gemma cried. "I don't want them to freeze to death in the snow." Gemma was almost in tears. Sean and Fluff were her favourite cockerel and hen.

"Don't worry Gem," said Karl. "Sean's clever. He'll keep them both safe."

"Yeah," added Meera. "Remember what Auntie Nat said about snow being a blanket? They'll cuddle up together under it, like Inuits in an igloo."

Gemma wasn't convinced, but it was impossible to look any more. They gave up the search and fought their way through the fast-flying snow to reach the safety of the farm office. They pulled the door shut behind them, relieved to be inside.

"Thank goodness!" said Flora. "I was just about to come and look for you." She looked pale and worried and made them sit by the stove to warm up.

"Drink this," Auntie Nat ordered, handing them mugs of soup. "You are very cold!"

They sat around the stove with the others and chatted. But soon their talk died down, drowned out by the wind howling and moaning outside, rattling every loose plank and tile.

"It sounds like something trying to get in." Meera shuddered.

No one replied. They all just huddled closer together in the flickering candlelight.

Chapter Four

In the middle of the night, Gemma woke up, worrying about Sean and Fluff. The little glow from the stove showed that everyone else was fast asleep. Squirt and Bish Bosh lay on one sofa, with Auntie Nat on the other and everyone else on airbeds and cushions on the floor. Even the dogs were asleep. Flinty was flopped across Flora's feet and Misty curled against Meera's back. Buster was doing a fine job as Karl's pillow.

Gemma sighed. She knew she should try to go back to sleep, but the thought of her favourite chooks out there in the snow wouldn't let her. She sat up and listened. The wind had definitely died down and moonlight showed through the windows. Perhaps she could just slip out quietly and look for them. She didn't want to wake any of the others, because they would tell her not to go. But she did want some company.

"Buster!" she breathed. "Buster!"

The old dog's keen ears heard her even in the middle of his rabbit-chasing dreams. With a soft "ruff", he wriggled out from under Karl's head without waking him and came over to Gemma, his tail wagging.

"Hello, boy," Gemma whispered. With Buster for company, she definitely felt brave enough to search for the chickens.

She pulled herself out of her sleeping bag and, as quietly as she could, squirmed into her boots and her outdoor clothes and grabbed Flora's headlamp from her desk. The office door was blocked with snow, but she managed to lever the top half of the stable door open with a broom, just enough to push Buster out and scramble after him. They landed in deep snow that came up to the top of Gemma's legs, and poor Buster completely disappeared! Gemma pushed hard with the broom, to make a path for both herself and the dog, and began to move in the direction of the ruined chicken house.

The wind had blown the snow into canyons and valleys which gleamed in the moonlight. Some snow was still falling, but the clouds were just scraps, racing in the navy-blue sky past the bright moon. The blizzard seemed to be over, at least for now.

But getting through the snow was slow going, and it was so thick that Gemma couldn't really tell if she'd got to the the ruins of the chicken house or not! And now the wind began to get up again, carrying the powdery snow into the air like mist.

Gemma stood still and listened, hoping to hear some giveaway clucks. But the only sound was the rising wind buffeting her ears. She was just about to give up and go back to the office when a very different sort of noise cut through the rushing air. The sound a donkey would make if it was practising opera – a high-pitched cross between a bray and a wheeze.

"Eeeeeeee, wurrr, eeee."

And it was coming from the far end of the

farm, where the alpacas had their house and pen.

"Eeeeewwwwrrrrr, hurrrrr, whhheeeee."

The sound was almost constant now. Gemma had heard Tika and Kusi making all sorts of funny noises – purring, humming and even a kind of "kersplatt" sound when they spat at somebody they didn't like – but never this. It didn't sound like a happy sort of noise. In fact, it sounded angry and frightened. Buster's fur bristled and he began to howl. She would have to go and investigate.

Gemma and Buster pushed through drift after drift that blocked their way to the end of the farm. All the while the wind got worse and the clouds gathered. By the time they reached the alpacas' pen, Flora's headlamp was like a sword of light cutting through the whirl of flakes.

Gemma could just make out that the door to the alpacas' sleeping quarters had blown open. Tika and Kusi were standing outside, shoulder to shoulder, making that strange noise and staring at something that was hidden between them and the fence around their pen. Now that she was closer, Gemma could hear that they were spitting at it too.

"Kersplatt. Kersplatt."

Gemma gripped her broom like a weapon and felt her heart beat hard enough to jump clean out of her chest. Buster's growl blossomed into a loud barking and Gemma was glad that her friend sounded so fierce and impressive. She began to wish that she had woken someone else, but it was too late to turn back now. Slowly she moved around the edge of the pen, until she could see what was causing all the fuss.

A wolf! Huge, bigger than an Alsatian dog, easily twice as big as Buster. But it wasn't behaving as Gemma expected a wolf to behave. It wasn't snarling or growling. In fact, it didn't look fierce at all. It was cowering with fear in front of the furious, spitting alpacas!

A wolf that was afraid of spitting alpacas probably wasn't much of a threat. But Buster wasn't so sure. He rushed to attack with a roaring bark. Seeing that someone had come to their rescue at last, the alpacas bolted back into their sleeping quarters. But in their excitement they forgot to go around Gemma and tried to go through her. She felt herself knocked flying. Then her head hit the metal bolt of the alpacas' door, everything went dark and the blizzard closed in.

Chapter Five

"Meera! Meera, wake up!" hissed Karl into Meera's ear.

Meera woke with a start, pushing Misty to one side as she sat up. "Wassamatter?"

"Shhh!" Karl whispered. "I don't want to wake Flora or Auntie Nat. They'll worry *and* they'll be cross."

Meera pushed the hair out of her eyes and tried to get her brain to work. All she could think about was how weird Karl's face looked, lit from underneath by his torch.

"Gemma's disappeared," Karl explained. "She's not anywhere inside. I think she's gone out looking for the lost chickens."

Suddenly, Meera was completely awake. "She's gone outside in *that*?" she said, pointing to the office windows where snow slooshed around like sheets in a washing machine.

"I don't think she's been gone long," said Karl. "Her sleeping bag's still a bit warm and she's taken Buster with her."

Karl didn't need to explain any more. In ten seconds, Meera was up, dressed and ready to go, with Misty sleepily wagging his tail beside her.

Together, the two children pushed open the top of the stable door. Snow squirted inside as if pushed by a high-pressure hose.

"Wait a minute," said Meera. "It's a white-out. We can't go out in that. We'll get lost. You can't see a thing."

They stood at the door, for a moment not knowing what to do.

Then Meera grinned. She tiptoed to Flora's desk and took a large ball of string from the bottom drawer. "We'll tie this to the door handle. Then we know we can find our way back."

Karl gave her a thumbs up and they pushed the door open and climbed out into the blizzard, leaving Misty whining faintly inside.

Meera held the string in one hand, and the end of Karl's scarf in the other. If she let go of either, she would be lost in moments. The snow was blowing in all directions, and it was so thick that she wondered if it was possible to drown in a blizzard.

"It's no good pointing the torch ahead," cried Karl. "I can't see a thing. But I can work out where we are if I point it downwards."

They scrubbed away at the snow with their feet to expose a tiny patch of ground to the torchlight.

"That's the brick path at the end of the yard," said Meera.

"She'll have gone towards where the chicken house was," Karl replied. "So we need to go right a bit now."

Their progress was so slow. It took ages to cover any distance and every few steps they had to check where they were by scrabbling under the snow for clues.

"Here's a bit of wood from the chicken

house," said Meera, digging with her boot as Karl shone the torch down. "But she could be anywhere!" Meera could hear the panic in her own voice.

"Maybe she's sheltering in the pigpen," suggested Karl. "It's over to our left."

But as they changed direction, Karl caught his foot on another piece of the chicken house under the snow. He fell, taking Meera with him, pulling the string out of her hand and sending the torch flying. It glowed briefly as it fell, then went out.

Karl and Meera helped each other up. It was very dark and the wind drove snow into their eyes and through every tiny gap in their clothing, stealing their warmth. This was no longer an adventure. Even though the safety of the Silver Street office was less than a hundred metres away, they might never find their way back without the string and the torch. They were lost in the snowstorm, just as Gemma was, and they knew they were in real danger.

"Which way do we go?" said Karl.

"I don't know!" Meera replied in a small voice.

They stood there, clinging to each other and wondering what to do, when suddenly they felt something moving around them, something alive. A big, furry dog-like creature. Meera would have run, but running in the drifting snow was impossible. She would have screamed, but she was too scared. With a low "ruff", the creature pressed itself against them.

Then Karl gasped. "It's pulling at my arm with its teeth!" he cried. "I think it wants us to go with it."

"Maybe it knows where Gemma is?" said Meera.

Bish Bosh poked his head out of the half-blocked door of the office.

The blizzard was dying down again and he could see scraps of starry sky through the cloud and snow.

Behind him was chaos as Flora and Auntie Nat panicked. They had woken to find that Meera, Karl and Gemma were missing and now they were preparing to go outside and search for them. Bish Bosh thought they were behaving like headless chickens. He couldn't see what all the fuss was about. "They're not stupid," he muttered to himself. "They'll be snuggled up with the sheep or something."

And then, as if to prove him right, some

shapes appeared out of the dark: Karl and Meera, with Gemma supported between them, and Buster and what looked rather like a wolf leading the way.

"They're here!" Bish Bosh called out over his shoulder. "Told you!"

Chapter Six

By the time Gemma, Karl and Meera had told the whole story of the spitting alpacas, the ball of string and the wolf rescue, it was morning.

"So Buster stayed with you, Gemma," said Flora. "And Wolfy here went to get help!" She pointed to the "wolf", who was now flopped like a doorstop at the entrance to the office.

"It was pretty scary when he came out of the blizzard!" said Karl. "But he took us to Gem, and Buster was lying on top of her like a blanket."

"*Wolf Heroes of Silver Street*," said Squirt, "would be a great movie." Now that Squirt was in the film business, he was always coming up with ideas for new blockbusters.

"Except that Buster isn't a wolf!" snapped Bish Bosh.

"Neither is that one," said Auntie Nat, narrowing her eyes over her mug of sweet tea and looking at the animal now gently snoring by the door. "Watch!"

Auntie Nat called out to the "wolf" in Russian. It woke immediately and came towards her, looking at her intently with its strange, ice-coloured eyes. She gave it another command and it sat in front of her, ears pricked and alert.

"No, not wolf." Auntie Nat smiled. "Highly trained Siberian sled dog! My uncle had dogs like this. Snow is their natural habitat."

The children were open-mouthed in amazement. A Russian-speaking sled dog on their doorstep was even more astonishing than a wolf.

"What is it doing *here*?" said Gemma from under the bandage round her head.

"Maybe it's wearing a collar," suggested Karl. "That could help us find out!"

Auntie Nat buried her fingers in the dog's thick neck fur and found a blue leather collar with silver writing on. It said Борис. "That is Boris, in Russian," she said, peering at the collar. "Ah, there is a telephone number here! I will call."

In a moment, Auntie Nat was on her mobile, talking very fast in Russian. When she came off the phone, she was beaming. But when the children asked her to explain, she just beamed some more. "You will see!" she said mysteriously. "Later!"

The blizzard was over and the snow lay under a huge blue sky. It was very cold, but not quite as far below zero as before. All the Silver Streeters – except Gemma, who was ordered not to move from her bed – wrapped up warm and went out to start their chores.

"Goodness!" exclaimed Flora, as they pushed their way through the drift over the door and stepped into the yard. "It's so beautiful!"

Any sign of the night's adventures had been buried under a new fall of snow and a different landscape of wind-blown drifts.

"I wish we could leave it like this!" said Meera.

"I do too," Flora replied. "But we need to clear the paths and pens so we can move around and the animals can have a bit of fresh air."

Bish Bosh handed out the shovels that he and Squirt had managed to get from the toolshed. "Right, let's get started!" Bish Bosh always liked using tools!

It was extremely hard work clearing away the snow, and everyone was soon very hot inside their layers of clothes. The dogs helped, digging enthusiastically, usually in the wrong place. Only Boris was really useful, digging efficiently exactly where he was asked.

"He is very happy," Auntie Nat said. "Snow is his home."

Gradually they worked their way across the farm, liberating animals from their sleeping quarters and letting them out into their snowy pens. Bobo and Bitzi looked bewildered, sniffing at the whiteness as if wondering where the grass had gone. The goats skipped round their pen, full of pent-up energy from a long time inside. But Mrs Fattybot was the funniest. The Gloucester Old Spot sow snuffled at the snow, sending little jets of it into the cold air. Then she ran round and round her pen like a little piglet.

But there was still no sign of Gemma's missing chickens and there was simply too much snow to clear to find them.

By the end of the afternoon, the paths were open all the way to the canal. Karl walked down with a bucket of food for the ducks and geese. As he stood watching the sun sink and the birds sliding on the ice, he heard a delicious shooshing sound coming down the canal towards him. Although he had never heard it before, he knew it was the sound of skates.

A moment later, a line of ten skaters appeared around the bend in the canal. Their fur hats and jackets looked like costumes, and the jewel colours of their clothes glowed in the sun. They were all wonderful skaters, moving effortlessly over the ice as if thinking about skating was just the same as doing it. Closer and closer they came, in a series of elegant curves. And then, in a whispering whoosh of skates, they stopped right in front of him. Karl breathed again, he realized he had been holding his breath since the skaters first appeared.

Their leader, a slender young woman in a scarlet coat, spoke up. "My name is Lena. This is Silver Street?" she said in an accent like Auntie Nat's. "You have my dog, Boris?"

Chapter Seven

It was a very full house at Silver Street for supper that evening. Not long after the skaters arrived, the children's old friends Sashi and Stewy from Cosmic TV, turned up on foot, dragging their camera equipment on a child's red plastic sled. They were in search of a story.

"There's nothing going on anywhere," Stewy complained. "So we thought we could at least film some pigs being cute in the snow."

"But it took so long to walk here pulling that little sled that now it's too dark to film!" Sashi said, rolling her eyes. "So who are all this lot?"

"They are the Siberian International Ballet!" said Meera. "They were on tour and they got stuck in Lonchester because of the snow..."

"...and then one of them lost their dog, 'cos it ran off into the snow, and we ... um, sort of found it," Karl concluded.

"Yesss!" said Sashi, punching the air. "I knew we'd get a story here. *Ballerina's Cute Chihuahua Gets Lost in Snow*!"

"Well," said Meera, "not quite. Lena's dog Boris is over there by the stove with Buster."

"Oh, boy!" Sashi gasped. "It's *huge*. What is it...?"

"Dunno," said Stewy, "but it's definitely not a chihuahua."

The larder at Silver Street mostly contained ingredients for cakes and biscuits to feed the Silver Street visitors, so the meal was a bit peculiar. But no one seemed to mind having three kinds of cake instead of a starter, main course and dessert, and eating it cross-legged on the floor. The ballet dancers loved it.

"At our hotel now," said Lena, licking carrot cake crumbs from her fingers, "just baked beans."

"Yes," added Dima, her dancing partner, "I think all people left in Lonchester living on baked beans!"

"That's true," said Sashi. "We've had calls from people all over the city who can't get to the shops and are running out of food."

Meera froze with a piece of cake halfway between her plate and her mouth. She looked at Boris, the sled dog, sitting like a guard behind Lena. She thought about Stewy's camera carried on the little red sled. She thought of all the Lonchester citizens who hadn't had an Uncle Sanjay to go to, who might be stranded in their cold houses with just a few tins of beans. And a big idea landed in her head with a pop so loud that she wondered if Karl and Gemma, sitting either side of her, had heard it.

"Lena," asked Meera, "do you think we could take a dog sled around the city, to deliver food?"

"Ah!" said Lena. "That is a good idea. A very fine idea. You are a smart girl, Meera."

Lena jumped up and did a little pirouette, then explained Meera's plan to the other dancers in a fast mixture of Russian and English. They all began talking at once and looked very pleased.

"Of course. We will all help," said Dima. "In the hotel, you know, it is very, very boring."

Tolya, the red-headed boy sitting next to Dima and one of the few dancers who spoke some English, said, "We all growed in Siberia. I am sledding with dogs when I was old three years."

"Wow," said Squirt, his eyes lighting up. "*Ballerina Dog Sledders*. That'd make such a good movie!"

"Don't think it's quite Hollywood, Squirt," said Sashi. "But it's perfect for Cosmic TV."

Chapter Eight

Early the next morning, the dancers from the Siberian International Ballet came skating back down the canal and were soon keeping their promise to help set up Lonchester's first dog-sled delivery service.

For people who looked as delicate and beautiful as a flock of elves, the dancers were amazingly practical. In no time at all they had swept the yard clear of snow to give themselves a work space. They raided the toolshed and the woodstore for materials to make a really big sled and, with help from a beaming Auntie Nat, filled the farm with Russian talk and songs.

"It's a bit like a blizzard, only of people not snow," Gemma said to Karl as they helped fetch and carry.

"I don't think I've ever seen Auntie so happy!" Karl replied.

Dima and Tolya led the sled-building team, whilst Lena got to work with the dogs.

"Does it matter that we only have one trained dog?" Meera asked.

Lena patted her dog's head. "My Boris is so brilliant, he will show the other dogs what to do." And she pointed at Flinty, Buster and Misty. "Today, we train these three dogs. But tomorrow, Meera, you must find four more. We must have eight."

"No problem!" Meera said, wondering where she was going to find four more dogs by the next day. She left Bish Bosh and Squirt in charge of making the reins – or traces as Lena called them – from baler twine, while she went inside to make some phone calls. There was a lot more than dogs to organize...

Lonchester Police Station – 9.15a.m.

Sergeant Short, Silver Street's special friend in the Lonchester police force, would never desert his city in a crisis. He had been at his desk for ten days without a rest, when Meera called with her strange request for help.

"Hmm," he said. "As this is an emergency, I think there are three police dogs coming up for retirement that I can let you borrow. And my dog, of course. Leave it with me. Regards to Flora and Auntie Nat."

Lonchester FM Radio Station – 1.14p.m.

Like Sergeant Short, Lonchester's most famous DJ, Rockin' Roland Rogers, was filling in for all the staff at Lonchester FM who had left town or were stranded by the snow. But he sounded only a little less chipper than ever on the lunchtime show.

"Hey there, snowy Lonchester," he drawled into the microphone. "Those crazy kids at Silver Street City Farm have had a great idea. They've teamed up with the visiting Russian ballet dancers to start ... now just wait to hear this ... Lonchester's first dog-sled delivery service. Good news for those of you down to your last tin of beans! It should be up and running ... or should I say *barking* ... very soon. They'll visit all of the city, district by district. Keep tuned in for news of when they're in your area... Next up, a track from Snow Paroles' new album *Frozen Solid*..."

Silver Street Farm — 3.53p.m.

Meera was amazed at how kind people could be. Even though Bobo and Bitzi, the naughty Silver Street sheep, had once run amok in his supermarket, Mr Morgan was very helpful.

"I've spoken to Head Office," he told Meera, "and they reckon that giving away some basic groceries is good publicity. And to be honest we've lost so much on sales in this weather that a few more pounds is neither here nor there. Let me know when you want to pick it all up, OK?"

4.20p.m.

Meera put the phone down and smiled.

"Success?" asked Flora, coming in from milking the goats.

"Yep!" said Meera. "I've got dogs, I've got publicity and I've got basic groceries – bread, tea, dried milk and cereal – to add to the Silver Street cheese."

Flora beamed. "That's brilliant. Well done! Now, take a look through the window. I think that's the rest of your sled team arriving."

Sliding into the yard on a pair of skis with a big smile on his face was Sergeant Short. With him were three German shepherd dogs and an enormous deerhound.

Two days later

"*Hike!*" said Lena. "*Hike! Hike!*"

Boris looked over his shoulder at his novice team, as if to say, "Come on guys! You heard the lady!" and threw his weight into the trace that connected him to the sled.

Beside Boris, his new best mate Buster pulled hard. Behind them, the three police dogs weren't *quite* sure what they were supposed to be doing, and Misty of course had no idea at all. But with Sergeant Short's deerhound, Yogi, to push them on and Flinty keen to nip their ankles if they didn't get on with it, they did what Lena asked. The sled with its trial load of five children took off and swept around the yard, past Stewy's camera. Everyone cheered.

"Oh, dear," said Dima to Auntie Nat in Russian. "It isn't exactly the most elegant sled. I wish we could have made something that looked better!"

Auntie Nat laughed. "Don't worry Dima. The team that's pulling it isn't exactly elegant either. But it will do the job."

Chapter
Nine

A week later, the Silver Street Dog-sled Delivery
Service had become a familiar sight all over the
city. And almost every day the service had run,
Karl had been on the sled, helping. He'd loved
taking food to people too old or sick to get out
in the snow. He'd loved the way people greeted
them with smiles and cheers. But his favourite
part of the day was the run home. He felt so
happy standing on the back of the sled with

Lena, whilst they sped over the snow and the dogs ran on in front of them.

They were nearly at that favourite part now. It was the last delivery of the afternoon. Soon they'd be heading back to Silver Street in an empty sled. Karl carried the bag of groceries into the old lady's kitchen. He was glad to see that she had a camping stove to cook on, but the house seemed very cold and the lady looked as fragile as a bird.

"Are you sure you'll be OK?" Karl asked her.

"Oh, bless you," she said, with a big crinkly smile. "I'm a lot tougher than I look and I'll be fine now I've got some food. Anyway, the freeze is going to end tomorrow. Haven't you heard the forecast?"

Karl walked back up the path to the waiting sled and dog team.

Dima was climbing on board. "Ah!" he said, snuggling down out of the wind. "I have carried too many boxes of beans today! I need your auntie's cakes!"

Karl got onto the back of the sled with Lena, as she urged the dogs on. They liked the run home too, with a light sled and the promise of a big bowl of food at the end of it.

"*Hike*!" Lena called again and clicked her tongue to make the dogs move faster. "Ah, they work just like a real team now!" she said to Karl, but he didn't reply. "Karl, you are so gloomy. What is it?"

"It's going to thaw tomorrow. Warmer weather's coming." Karl felt like he might cry.

"Ah, I see," sighed Lena. "And you like this snow and the sled very much, don't you?"

Karl just nodded.

"I will miss this team of dogs and people too," said Lena, quietly. "I never could decide if I like dancing or dog-sledding best." She handed him the traces. "You drive," she said, with a smile. "You give them their orders, Karl. They will go faster for you."

Karl's eyes shone in the sunset, he clicked his tongue and the dogs flew over the white world to Silver Street.

If the weather forecast was right, the airport would be open by the morning. The Siberian International Ballet and their mascot, Boris the sled dog, would be leaving Lonchester. The Silver Street Dog-sled Delivery Service would no longer be needed and life would be back to boring normal.

Nobody at Silver Street was pleased.

"I not want to leave Auntie Nat's carrot cake," said Tolya.

"Or cute pigs. I am in love with Mrs Fattybot," said Pavel.

"I like being at Silver Street!" wailed Bish Bosh. "I don't wanna go back to school!"

"I like now the ugly sled we made!" said Dima. "I also *love* the ugly dog team," he added in Russian, so no one would be offended.

Auntie Nat smiled and thought how much she was going to miss speaking Russian.

Stewy and Sashi came by to take shots of the last dog-sled day and Sergeant Short popped by on his skis to collect the dogs.

Everyone was pretty gloomy until Auntie Nat called them into the office. "I have made special five-cake dinner," she announced, "to thank our friends."

"And I would like to announce," said Lena, jumping nimbly onto a chair, "that we will make a ballet about Silver Street and our adventures in the snow with you!"

After that, everyone cheered up. There was a lot of singing and laughing. Olga taught Sergeant Short, Squirt and Bish Bosh how to partner a ballerina. Dima found that he and Auntie Nat had been to the same school, although at very different times. Flora showed Tolya and Pavel a Scottish dance with lots of jumps in it. And Maxim and Gemma found that they'd both once hatched ducklings in their bedrooms.

But Karl was only pretending to have a good time. Inside, his heart sank. While the whole room was learning another of Flora's Highland flings, Lena came and spoke to him quietly. She led him outside. The sky was still clear and bright and the waning moonlight gleamed on the snow. It was bright enough to see without a torch.

"The ice will melt," said Lena, "but not yet. Now it is like a ballroom floor." She handed him a pair of skates and took him down to the canal.

Karl wobbled at first, but not for long.

"You were born to it, Karl!" said Lena. "Ah! Now here come the others!"

All the ballet dancers trooped down to the canal with their ice skates. They were carrying torches that looked like huge candles as they burned and flickered red and orange. They had one for Karl.

Up and down the canal they skated, through the last night of the snowy world.

They held their torches high and swooped and curved to make fiery patterns in the darkness, until at last a soft, warm rain quenched the flames.

Chapter Ten

The next afternoon, Meera, Karl and Gemma stood at the edge of the canal, watching the last bits of ice bob about under the falling rain.

"Well," said Meera, "at least the ducks are happy."

"And Chinook!" said Gemma. "Look!"

The Canada goose was ruffling her feathers and flapping her wings, splashing water everywhere, clearly very pleased indeed

that the world had been restored to proper liquid order.

"Didn't take long to melt, did it?" said Karl sadly.

"There are still huge lumps of snow everywhere, though," Meera said brightly, trying to make Karl feel a bit better.

"I wonder if we'll ever find out what happened to Fluff and Sean," Gemma wondered wistfully.

"Gemma! Meera! Karl!" Squirt's piercing little voice called from where the old signal box had been.

"Yeah, get over here!" Bish Bosh added. "You'll never guess who's just walked out from under the snow."

The three friends raced to where the brothers stood by the ruins of the chicken house, still half-covered by a hump of dirty snow.

"Must have been trapped in there with the grain bin, I reckon," said Bish Bosh.

"And pecked the snow for water," said Squirt.

There, picking their way through the snow and the ruins of their old home, were Sean and his lady, Fluff. Gemma squealed. She was so happy she actually jumped up and down. She looked so funny with her ginger plaits flying and her wellies dancing that Karl found a giggle rising like a bubble in his sad heart. It burst out of him and was caught at once by the other children.

Then it seemed to Karl that a smile spread across the whole farm, touching the animals and the buildings, and the sprouting clumps of snowdrops. And Karl was suddenly reminded that even the coldest winters are followed by spring.

SILVER STREET FARM

The Little Farm in the Big City

WELCOME TO
SILVER STREET FARM

NICOLA DAVIES

ESCAPE FROM
SILVER STREET FARM

NICOLA DAVIES

SPRING FEVER AT
SILVER STREET
FARM

NICOLA DAVIES

ALL ABOARD AT
SILVER STREET
FARM

NICOLA DAVIES

CROWDED OUT AT
SILVER STREET
FARM

NICOLA DAVIES

FROZEN SOLID AT
SILVER STREET
FARM

NICOLA DAVIES